S0-BZM-474

# Jorge and the Lost Cookie Jar

by Marta Arroyo

illustrated by Penny Weber

 **Dayton Publishing** • Solana Beach California

Text set in Tuff (Stone Type Foundry)
Labels on illustrations set in BrookeShappell8 (FontSpace)

Printed and bound in USA

Dayton Publishing LLC
Solana Beach, CA 92075
858-775-3629
publisher@daytonpublishing.com
www.daytonpublishing.com

ISBN-13: 978-0-9970032-4-6

For my dear grandchildren, Irene, Jacob, Cruz, Grace, and Nora
— M. A.

For Nonni and her yummy oatmeal-raisins
— P. W.

This story contains a sprinkling of Spanish words and phrases, which appear in blue. If you need help pronouncing them, or understanding what they mean, check the "Glossary" at the back of the book.

One chilly autumn weekend, **Jorge** and his brother and sisters moved into their new home with their mother and father, grandmother and grandfather.

Gracie's room

Lola's room

Porch

Abuelo and Abuelita's room

Jorge and Cruz's room

kitchen

garage

After a long morning of household chores and unpacking, the family had a quick lunch. Then they went back to emptying boxes.

Jorge and his brother, Cruz, were working in their room. Before long Jorge was in the mood for a cookie break. Cookies were Jorge's favorite afternoon snack — delicious, homemade galletas baked with love by Mamá and Abuelita.

"Cruz, have you seen the cookie jar?"
Jorge asked his brother.

Cruz was unpacking boxes of puzzles
and games.

"No," he said, "I haven't seen it.
But bring me a cookie if you find it,
por favor."

Jorge started toward the stairs to go down to the kitchen. On the way he passed his sister Lola's door.

He stopped and looked in, but there was no cookie jar in sight.

"Lola, have you seen the cookie jar?" he asked.

"Look on the kitchen counter," Lola said. "Mamá must have unpacked it by now."

Jorge went downstairs.

In the kitchen Jorge saw some empty jars and a big pitcher filled with wooden cooking spoons. But there was no cookie jar in sight.

"Mamá, where is el jarro de galletas?" he asked.

Mamá gave him a kiss.

"It's not here, mijo. I haven't seen it.
Maybe Gracie has it."

Jorge went back upstairs.

In Gracie's room he saw a wicker basket filled with books and magazines, **but no cookie jar.**

"Gracie, do you know where the cookie jar is?" Jorge asked.

Gracie only shrugged. "Ask Mamá," she said.

"But I *already asked* Mamá," said Jorge. "She doesn't know! Oh, now where will we keep the chocolate chip cookies?  They're my favorite!"

Jorge turned around and went down the stairs again. He headed for the garage, where Papá was working.

He saw Papá with his toolbox and a chest of plastic drawers. But there was still no cookie jar.

"Papá, where is the cookie jar?" Jorge asked.

"I don't have it, mijo," said Papá.

"Well . . . now where will we keep the polvorones?" Jorge asked. "Mamá makes those the *best*..."

"Oh, I know!" he said.
"I'll ask Abuelita."

Jorge found Abuelita watering plants on the porch.
But still there was no cookie jar.

"Abuelita, have you seen the cookie jar?" said Jorge.
"I'm hungry for a cookie!"

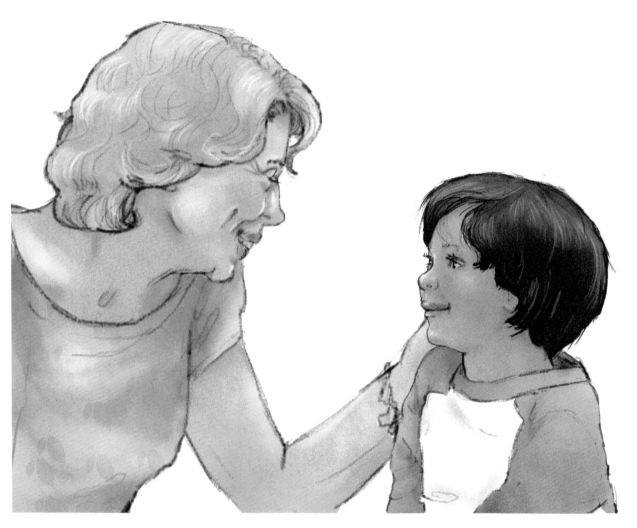

"No, mijo," she replied. "Go inside and ask your Abuelo. Maybe he has it. I think I remember that he packed it. You will find it. And when you do, I'll bake you some fresh galletas!"

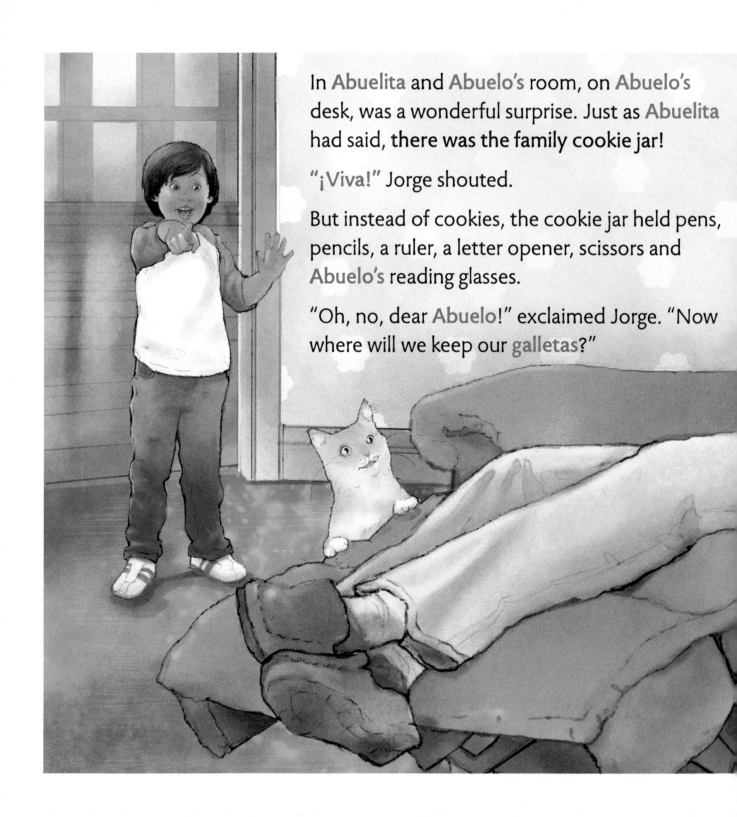

In Abuelita and Abuelo's room, on Abuelo's desk, was a wonderful surprise. Just as Abuelita had said, there was the family cookie jar!

"¡Viva!" Jorge shouted.

But instead of cookies, the cookie jar held pens, pencils, a ruler, a letter opener, scissors and Abuelo's reading glasses.

"Oh, no, dear Abuelo!" exclaimed Jorge. "Now where will we keep our galletas?"

"I'm sorry, mijo," said Abuelo. "Let's empty out this cookie jar. I can find something else to hold my writing supplies. And let's go to la cocina to bake some cookies right now."

"Si, Abuelo. Abuelita will help us!  I wonder what we should bake  —  polvorones . . . ? chocolate chip cookies . . . ? sugar cookies . . . ? I can hardly wait till they come out of the oven!

"Gracias, Abuelo."

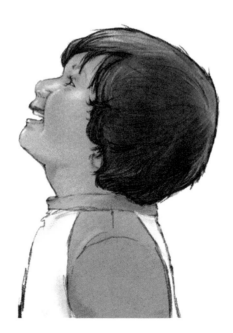

Papá       Gracie       Mamá

Everyone agreed, the cookies were delicious.

Lola     Cruz     Abuelo     Jorge     Abuelita

# Glossary

**Abuela** (a•BWEH•la) means **Grandmother.**
  **Abuelita** (a•bweh•LEE•ta) can be used to show special affection.

**Abuelo** (a•BWEH•lo) means **Grandfather.**
  **Abuelito** (a•bweh•LEE•to) can be used to show special affection.

**Cruz** (CROOZ)

**el jarro de galletas** (ell harro deh ga•YEH•tahs) means **the cookie jar.**

**galletas** (gah•YEH•tahs) means **cookies.**

**gracias** (GRAH•see•ahs) means **thank you.**

**Jorge** (HOR•heh)

**la cocina** (la ko•SEE•na) means **the kitchen.**

**Mamá** (ma•MA) means **Mama, Mom, or Mommy.**

**mijo** (MEE•ho) is a contraction of **mi hijo** (mee•EE•ho)  It is an affectionate way of saying **my son.** Likewise, **mija** (MEE•ha), for **mi hija,** means **my daughter.** But either can also be used for someone who is not your son or daughter, as a colloquial term of endearment.

**Papá** (pa•PA) means **Papa, Dad, or Daddy.**

**polvorones** (pol•bo•RO•nehs) are heavy, soft, crumbly cookies made from flour, sugar, milk, and nuts. Another name for them is **Mexican wedding cookies.** This type of cookie originated in Spain and is popular in Latin America and the Philippines.

**por favor** (por•fa•VOR) means **please.**

**¡Viva!** (VEE•va) means **Hooray!** (In Spanish, exclamations and questions have their punctuation marks both before and after them.)

# About the Author

 **Marta Arroyo** graduated from the University of California at Santa Barbara, where she majored in Spanish Literature. She taught in the elementary grades for more than 30 years, primarily in the Carlsbad Unified School District. Since her retirement she has written two bilingual children's books, *La Fiesta y el Mariachi* (2007) and *The Story of Señora Tamales* (2010). *Jorge and the Lost Cookie Jar* is her first book with Dayton Publishing. Marta lives in Oceanside, California, with her husband, Juan. Her passion is playing games with her grandchildren. She also volunteers at their schools and is available to read in local classrooms and libraries.

# About the Illustrator

 **Penny Weber** is a full-time artist and illustrator from Long Island, New York, where she has lived all her life. She works both digitally and traditionally in acrylics and watercolors. Penny attended classes at the School of Visual Arts in Manhattan. In 2007 she turned her attention to children's book illustration and since has illustrated many books, including the *Chris P. Bacon* series. Some of Penny's clients are Hay House, McGraw-Hill Education, Seed Learning, Tilbury House, and Learning A–Z. *Jorge and the Lost Cookie Jar* is her first book with Dayton Publishing. Penny has a husband, three children, and a cat.

Jorge and Kitty searched the house for the lost cookie jar.
Can you follow their path? Kitty will help you.

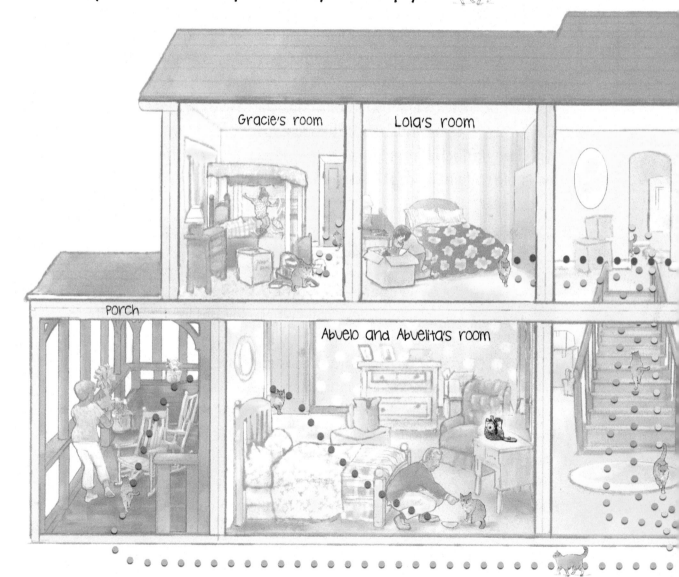

Jorge and Cruz's room

- • • • They started in Jorge and Cruz's room, and they went to Lola's room.
- • • • They went downstairs to the kitchen.
- • • • Then they went up the stairs and along the back hall to Gracie's room.
- • • • Next they went down to the garage.
- • • • Then they went to the porch,
- • • • and then into Abuelo and Abuelita's room.

**And there was the cookie jar!**

garage

kitchen

CPSIA information can be obtained
at www.ICGtesting.com
Printed in the USA
LVOW06*2321010118
561475LV00016B/39/P